S0-ATP-911

DISCARDED

Lily and
Miss Liberty

Lily and Miss Liberty

by CARLA STEVENS

illustrated by

DEBORAH KOGAN RAY

SCHOLASTIC INC.

New York   Toronto   London   Auckland   Sydney

If you purchased this book without a cover, you should be aware that this book is stolen property. It was reported as "unsold and destroyed" to the publisher, and neither the author nor the publisher has received any payment for this "stripped book."

No part of this publication may be reproduced in whole or in part, or stored in a retrieval system, or transmitted in any form or by any means, electronic, mechanical, photocopying, recording, or otherwise, without written permission of the publisher. For information regarding permission, write to Scholastic Inc., 730 Broadway, New York, NY 10003.

ISBN 0-590-44920-6

Text copyright © 1992 by Carla Stevens.
Illustrations copyright © 1992 by Debra Kogan Ray.
All rights reserved. Published by Scholastic Inc.
APPLE PAPERBACKS is a registered trademark of Scholastic Inc.

12 11 10 9 8 7 6   5 6 7/9

Printed in the U.S.A.   40

For Eddie
C.S.

CONTENTS

Lily and
Miss Liberty

I
The Present from France

It was almost time for supper. Grandma was feeding baby Charlie, and Mama was cooking cabbage on the big coal-burning stove. After Lily set the table, she went into the parlor to read the book she had brought from school.

Papa was sitting in his favorite armchair, reading a magazine.

"Look, Lily," he said. "Look at the picture of the French ship that is bringing the Statue of Liberty to New York. It is due here in just a few more days."

Lily sat on the arm of Papa's chair and peered at the picture in the magazine. "But where is Miss Liberty?" she asked. "I don't see her."

"Below deck, packed in hundreds of boxes," Papa replied. "It will be some time before we can see her. First we have to build the pedestal for her to stand on."

"Mama doesn't like Miss Liberty," Lily said.

Mr. Lafferty put down his magazine. "Oh, I'm sure she does."

"No, she doesn't," Lily insisted. "She says we shouldn't have to pay for it."

"We don't have to pay for the statue, Lily. The statue is a gift from France," Papa said. "We only have to raise enough money to pay for the pedestal."

"But she says the pedestal will cost a lot of money. She thinks we should use our money to help feed poor people instead."

Mr. Lafferty picked up his magazine again. "Goodness, Lily, why bother your head about all this?"

"Our class is raising money for the pedestal and I didn't put in anything again today," Lily said. "I was almost the only one."

"Well, well, Lily, that's a problem, isn't it."

"Supper is ready!" called Mrs. Lafferty.

Lily and Papa went into the kitchen. Lily sat down at the big round table next to

Grandma. Mama began dishing out the corned beef and cabbage.

Papa took a bite of cabbage. "Mmm. What a good cook you are, Mama!"

Mrs. Lafferty smiled at her husband.

"Lily tells me that her class is raising money for Miss Liberty's pedestal," he said. "Can't we think of some way for Lily to earn a little money, too?"

Mama set her mouth in a straight line. "All the poor people living in this city! No one thinks of raising money to help them!"

"I know, I know," Papa said. "But what a wonderful statue Miss Liberty is! And someday soon she will stand in our harbor to welcome all the immigrants like ourselves who have come to America seeking a better life and the freedom to enjoy it."

"Humpf," Mama said. "You talk about freedom. But freedom won't fill an empty stomach."

"Sometimes freedom is more important than an empty stomach, Mama."

"You don't remember what it feels like to be hungry, Papa. I remember."

Grandma glanced at Lily. "All this talk isn't helping Lily," she said. "How is she going to earn money for Miss Liberty's pedestal?"

"Maybe you can help Mrs. Casella in her grocery store," Papa suggested.

"Or maybe you could help Otto, the super, sweep the front steps of our apartment building," Grandma said.

Papa pushed back his chair and stood up. "That was a good dinner, Mama." He turned to Lily. "Tomorrow is Saturday. I'm sure you will find something to do for Miss Liberty, Lily."

After Lily helped Grandma dry the supper dishes, she went outside and sat down on the front steps. Although it was almost eight o'clock, it had not yet begun to grow dark. Wagons and carriages passed back and forth on the cobblestoned street. A peddler walked by pushing his empty cart. Two boys were playing marbles on the sidewalk next door.

Suddenly she spotted her friend Rachel across the street, pulling a little dog behind her.

Lily ran to greet her. "Hi, Rachel. Where did you get the dog?"

"Hi, Lily. Olga belongs to Mrs. Volinski. She's going to give me ten cents if I walk her every night for a week." Rachel looked pleased with herself. "More money for Miss Liberty!"

"Oh," Lily said.

Rachel looked at Lily curiously. "How come you haven't brought in any money yet?"

"I had to mind Charlie again yesterday. So I had no time to look for a job." Lily hesitated before adding, "And besides, my mother doesn't like the Statue of Liberty so much."

"She doesn't? Poor you!" Rachel exclaimed.

"But I love Miss Liberty," Lily said quickly. "And so does Papa."

"So do I! And do you know what?"

"What?" Lily asked.

"I'm French!"

Lily glared at Rachel. "You are not!"

"Oh, yes I am. That's what my mama says. My name is French."

"It is not."

"Yes, it is. My mama told me so."

"Lily is French, too."

"It is not."

5

"I say it is a hundred times!" Lily shouted angrily.

"And I say it isn't two hundred times!" Rachel shot back, and she took off down the sidewalk pulling the dog behind her.

Lily crossed the street and ran up the steps into her building. She ran up another flight of stairs to her apartment and burst into the kitchen.

"Why, Lily, what's the matter?" Mrs. Lafferty asked when she saw her.

"I have a French name, don't I, Mama?" Lily asked breathlessly.

"Lily, you know perfectly well you are named after my older sister who still lives in Ireland."

"But I could be French if I wanted to, couldn't I?" Lily persisted. "Rachel says her name is French, but mine isn't."

Mrs. Lafferty gave Lily a hug. "Your name is just as French as hers is, Lily dear. Now get along to bed. Tomorrow is going to be a busy day for you."

Lily looked at her mother. "Do you really

think I can earn some money for Miss Liberty's pedestal, Mama?"

"Yes, Lily. But it won't be easy. There are many people who don't think as much of that statue as you and Papa do."

When Lily fell asleep that night, she dreamed that a beautiful lady stopped her carriage in front of her building.

"Are you Lily Lafferty?" she asked.

"Yes," Lily replied.

"Here is something for the Pedestal Fund." And she handed Lily a whole dollar!

Lily couldn't help but notice that the lady wore a crown that looked just like Miss Liberty's.

2
Two Pennies and a Lollipop

❧

When Lily awoke the next morning, her grandmother was getting dressed to go to work.

"Stay in bed, Lily. You don't have to get up so early. Today is Saturday," Grandma said.

"Don't you remember, Grandma? Today I have to earn money for Miss Liberty."

"Liberty, Liberty, that's all the ladies at the shop talk about. They say rich people should pay for the pedestal. I say we should pay for the pedestal, too. That way the statue will belong to all of us."

"You said that, Grandma?"

"I said it and I mean it."

"Oh, Grandma, I love you!"

After breakfast, Lily went downstairs and out onto the sidewalk. She could tell that it was going to be a warm day. The street sprinkler was coming up the street, pulled slowly by an old white horse. Sprays of water were coming out of the bottom of the tank and wetting the dusty cobblestones.

Mr. Ames was sitting on top of the big tank under his umbrella. "So, Lily! Nice day, eh?"

Lily walked alongside the tank, feeling the tickle of the spray on her legs. "Do you know any work I could do, Mr. Ames?"

"You're too young to work, Lily. Get back now, you're going to get wet."

"But I want to earn money for Miss Liberty's pedestal," Lily said.

"Why don't rich people pay for it? Those money kings are too tightfisted, that's why." Mr. Ames slapped the reins and the old horse began to trot down the street.

Lily turned back. First she would look for Otto, who lived in a basement apartment two buildings down the block. He was just coming up the steps as Lily reached his house.

"Otto, can I help you sweep the sidewalk?"

"What for, Lily? Sweeping is one of my jobs."

"But I need to earn some money," Lily said.

"Is it money you want? I have no money to spare, little lady. I have too many mouths to feed."

It's true about the mouths, Lily thought. Mr. and Mrs. Dorfman have six children.

Lily headed for Mr. Kaminsky's apartment. He lived four houses down from Otto's building on the first floor. Mr. Kaminsky came to the door when Lily knocked.

"Would you like me to walk your dog for you today, Mr. Kaminsky?"

"No, no, Lily. This is a beautiful day and I need the exercise. Come again when it rains," Mr. Kaminsky said, closing the door.

Lily walked back toward her house. She still hadn't tried Mrs. Casella's grocery store. Just as she was passing her building, her mother leaned out of the window.

"Lily, Mrs. Rosen isn't feeling well. Will you bring her some chicken soup? I don't want to leave Charlie alone."

"Yes, Mama." Lily went upstairs to get the soup. When she reached Mrs. Rosen's apartment, she rang the bell.

A faint voice answered. "Who's there?"

Lily opened the door. "It's me, Lily."

Mrs. Rosen was lying in bed. "I don't feel so well today," she said.

"Here is some soup my mama made, Mrs. Rosen." Lily put the bowl on the table near the bed and turned to go.

"Oh, Lily, could you go to Mrs. Casella's and get me a bottle of milk and six eggs?" Mrs. Rosen reached for her purse. "Here is the money."

Lily closed Mrs. Rosen's door and headed down the block toward Mrs. Casella's grocery store. Just as she was passing Seymour's butcher shop she heard, "Oh, Lily, you've come by just in time. Will you do me a favor and mind Sheila while I go in to get some chicken?" It was her mother's friend, Mrs. Murphy.

Mrs. Murphy didn't wait for Lily's answer. She opened the butcher shop door and went inside, leaving Lily with Sheila in her carriage.

The minute Mrs. Murphy disappeared into the butcher shop, Sheila began to cry.

Lily leaned over the carriage and tried to make a funny face. But Sheila cried even louder.

"What did you do to your little sister?"
asked a woman who was passing by.

"She's not my sister," Lily said, knocking
on the window of the butcher shop to get
Mrs. Murphy's attention. Mrs. Murphy waved.
Sheila cried even louder.

An old woman stopped and shook her head.
"Tsk, tsk, tsk."

At last Mrs. Murphy came out. When Sheila saw her mother she stopped crying and began to smile.

"What a good girl you are, Sheila!" said Mrs. Murphy. Then she turned to Lily. "Thank you, dear. Here's a lollipop for you and one for Sheila."

Lily wished it were a nickel instead, but she thanked Mrs. Murphy and continued on to the grocery store.

When Lily arrived at Mrs. Casella's, she saw her friend, Dino, behind the counter. Her heart sank. "Hi, Dino. What are you doing here?"

"I'm working for Mrs. Casella," Dino said.

"Does she need anyone else, do you think?" Lily asked timidly.

"Oh, no," Dino replied quickly. "She only needs one helper and that's me."

Lily bought the eggs and milk and hurried back to her building.

Mrs. Rosen was sitting up in bed. "Thank you, dear," she said. She reached over to get her purse on the table. "Here, Lily. For you."

Lily looked at the two pennies Mrs. Rosen offered her. "Thank you, Mrs. Rosen. Well, I'd better be going now."

Lily slowly climbed the stairs to her apartment. Mama was right. It was going to be much harder to earn money than she had thought. Two pennies and a lollipop! That was not enough money to bring to school on Monday. What was she going to do?

3
Fourteen Crowns

Sunday morning, Lily woke to the good smells of biscuits baking and bacon frying. She could see into the kitchen from her bed. Grandma was leaning over the stove while Mama was feeding Charlie. How will I ever earn money for Miss Liberty on a Sunday? she asked herself.

"Hurry and get dressed, Lily, or we'll be late for church," Mama said.

Lily got out of bed and began to put on her Sunday clothes.

Soon after breakfast, the Laffertys headed down their block to the church on the corner.

Once inside, Lily sat quietly in a pew between Mama and Grandma. Two ladies in the pew in front of her wore big flowery hats with wide brims. They blocked Lily's view.

I'm glad Miss Liberty doesn't wear a big hat,

Lily thought. A crown is much, much better. That must be why queens wear crowns instead of hats.

Suddenly Lily sat up straight. What if she could make some crowns just like the one Miss Liberty wears! Then she could sell them to people and make money for the pedestal! But what could she make the crowns out of? And how would they fit?

Lily began to wriggle impatiently. If only she could whisper her idea to Grandma. Mama put her hand on Lily's lap to quiet her.

At last the service came to an end. As soon as they were out on the street, Lily burst out, saying, "Grandma! What if I could make some crowns just like the one Miss Liberty wears and sell them!"

"Crowns. Crowns. Hmm. Let me think." Grandma was quiet for a moment. "Why, Lily, I think you've got a good idea!"

"But what could we make them out of, Grandma?"

Grandma turned to Papa and Mama. "Lily wants to make Liberty crowns and sell them for the Pedestal Fund."

"Crowns. Hmm. What could she make a crown out of?" Papa wondered.

"Something that wouldn't be too hard to cut with scissors," Mama said.

"Stiff, but not too stiff," Grandma added.

As soon as they arrived back home, Lily went into the front room and began searching through Mama's sewing shelf for some material that might be used for Miss Liberty's crown. There were lengths of velvet and wool, cotton and linen, ribbons and yarn, but nothing seemed right.

Lily sighed. "I can't find anything."

"I know what you can make them out of," Papa said. "I'll be back soon." And he left the apartment.

Grandma began sorting through the fabrics on the shelf. She pulled out a small piece of stiff material that Mama used to make her hats. "First we need a pattern. You can make a pattern out of this piece of buckram."

"But how will I know how big to make the crown?" Lily asked.

Grandma took a piece of ribbon from her sewing basket and put it around Lily's head.

"That's how big you have to make the crown, Lily," she said. "After you make the crown, we will poke two holes in the back. We will attach two long strings to the holes so that the crown can be tied around anyone's head."

Lily took the ribbon and laid it along the length of the buckram. Then she drew the rays that extended from the crown.

"Miss Pearson told us they are supposed to be the rays of the sun shining on the seven seas and seven continents of the world," Lily said.

Lily had to draw the rays four times before

they looked like the ones on Miss Liberty's crown.

"Sometimes you have to try and try again until you get something right," Grandma said.

The door opened. It was Papa. "Jack Reilly

prints posters on this paper," he said. "Jack made a present of this to you. I think it will be just the right stiffness for your crowns, Lily."

Lily looked at the big sheets of yellow paper Papa put on the kitchen table. "Oh, thank you, Papa!"

Lily cut out a crown following the pattern she had made. After she cut it out, she poked two holes in the back for the string. Then she folded the rays down so that they extended out from her forehead.

At last Lily tried it on. She ran to look in the mirror. Yes, it did look like Miss Liberty's crown!

When Grandma saw Lily, she smiled. "I think people will buy your crowns."

Lily and Grandma and Mama cut out crown after crown.

When Lily counted them, she could hardly believe they had made so many. Fourteen crowns! And there were still some sheets of paper left for more crowns.

"Can I sell them now?" she asked.

"Wait until the afternoon. People like to

take a stroll after Sunday dinner," Papa suggested.

"How much will your crowns cost?" Mama asked.

"Not so much that people won't buy them, and not too little so that you won't make much money for Miss Liberty," Papa said.

"So how much, then?" Lily asked impatiently.

Grandma was listening from the bedroom. "I think fifteen cents."

"Oh, no!" exclaimed Mama. "That's way too much for people to pay. I think five cents."

Lily thought about her crowns. She would never be able to buy one for fifteen cents. That was a lot of money. But five cents seemed too little. "I think I will charge ten cents," she said.

She sprawled out on her bed with a pencil and paper and tried to think of what she could say to make people stop and buy her crowns.

She decided to write a poem.

"Miss Liberty is sailing across the sea,
A present from France to you and me,
The boat that brings her will soon reach
   our land,
But we can't see her 'til she has a place to
   stand."

Lily didn't have much room left on the
sheet of paper. She wrote, *Buy a crown and
help to pay for Miss Liberty's ped—* Lily looked
up. "How do you spell 'pedestal'?"

"P-e-d-e-s-t-a-l," Mama said.

After Lily wrote *pedestal,* she added *ten cents*
and then signed her name, *Lily Lafferty.*

"I'm finished," she said. She was ready to
sell the crowns at last!

4
Crowns for Sale!

After dinner, Papa and Grandma helped Lily carry the crowns downstairs. Papa placed two wooden crates on the sidewalk. Then he put a plank across to make a shelf. He nailed Lily's sign to the front of the plank.

"Good luck, Lily," Grandma said as she and Papa went back up to the apartment.

Lily arranged her crowns on the plank. Only eight would fit so she put the rest on the front step beside her. She sat down and waited. Suddenly she remembered something. People would want to see themselves with their crowns on! She ran upstairs to get her little mirror.

Lily was just putting on one of her crowns when Mr. Kaminsky walked by with his dog.

"My, you look pretty today, Lily. Are you a princess?"

"No, Mr. Kaminsky. I am selling crowns for

Miss Liberty's pedestal. Would you like to buy one?"

"Oh, no, thank you. It wouldn't fit my head."

"But I made them so they fit everybody," Lily said eagerly.

"How about if I give you five cents and you keep the crown." Mr. Kaminsky pulled some money out of his pocket.

"Thank you," Lily said, but she was disappointed. She watched Mr. Kaminsky continue down the street with his dog.

Mrs. Rosen stuck her head out of the window. "I'm much better," she called. "I'm up and about again."

Lily smiled. "That's good, Mrs. Rosen. Would you like to buy a crown?"

"What for?" Mrs. Rosen asked.

"It's for Miss Liberty's pedestal."

"Ugh. That statue. Who wants it, I want to know," Mrs. Rosen said as she withdrew from the window.

"I do, Mrs. Rosen," Lily said softly, but Mrs. Rosen was gone.

Horses and carriages passed up and down

the street, but no one seemed to be looking her way. Several people walked by but they didn't stop. Now Jo O'Grady was coming toward her, pushing a baby carriage. Lily looked at her hopefully. "Would you like to buy a crown?" she asked.

Jo picked up a crown and put it on.

"Ooh, you look pretty," Lily said, admiring Jo's bright red hair piled on top of her head.

Jo peered at herself in Lily's mirror. "How much?" she asked.

"Ten cents." Lily held her breath.

"All right," Jo O'Grady said. "It's for a good cause." She gave Lily ten cents and put the crown in the carriage.

Lily wondered why she didn't wear it.

Just then, Lily spotted Rachel coming toward her from across the street.

"What are those?" Rachel asked, pointing at the crowns.

"They're crowns, like the one on Miss Liberty."

"How come you made so many?"

"I'm selling them to get money for the pedestal," Lily said. "They're ten cents each."

"Can I try one on?"

Lily handed her the crown she had on her head.

Rachel put it on. "Let me see how I look." She peered at herself in the mirror. "Not bad," she said.

"You can have it," Lily said impulsively.

"But I don't have ten cents," Rachel said.

"That's all right. You can still have it."

"Thanks." Rachel paused. "You know what?"

"What?" Lily asked.

"I'm not French like I said."

Lily looked surprised. "You're not?"

"My mother said I'm Polish."

"You know what?" Lily said. "I'm not French, either. I'm named after my aunt in Ireland."

"But we could pretend to be French, couldn't we?" Rachel said. *"Bonjour.* That means 'good morning.' "

Lily put on another crown. *"Bonjour,"* she said.

Rachel stood on the sidewalk in front of Lily's stand. "I think we should yell to get

people to stop. We can yell together."

Lily grinned at her best friend. Selling crowns with Rachel was going to be fun.

"Crowns for sale!" they yelled. "Ten cents a crown! A crown to help Miss Liberty!"

A fancy carriage pulled by two black horses stopped in front of the stand. A lady leaned out of the window. "A crown, did you say? I'll take two for my daughters."

Rachel raced up to the carriage with two crowns and handed them to the lady. "Thanks," she said when she received the dimes.

As the carriage moved on, Rachel ran out into the street and began yelling, "Crowns for sale! Buy a crown for Miss Liberty!"

By five o'clock, all the crowns were sold. When they counted the money, they had made one dollar and thirty-five cents.

"That wasn't so hard, was it," Rachel said cheerfully. "See you in school tomorrow, Lily."

Lily watched Rachel skip across the street holding onto the crown perched on her head. Imagine making all that money for Miss Liberty's pedestal! Won't Mama be surprised!

5
The Fund Grows Bigger

Lily could hardly contain her excitement as she headed for school Monday morning. Pinned on her dress was the little purse Mama had given her to carry all the money—one dollar and thirty-seven cents.

When she arrived at school, she spotted Rachel waiting for her on the sidewalk, wearing her crown.

"Hi, Rachel!" she said when she caught up with her.

"What's that thing you've got on your head?" someone yelled.

"None of your business!" Rachel yelled back.

Lily looked at her friend admiringly. She wished she had the nerve to talk back to those older boys.

Rachel pointed to a girl who was standing
by herself near the front gate of the school.
"What's the matter with her?"

Lena Koslov was crying. Did one of the big
boys hit her?

Rachel grabbed Lily's hand and pulled her
toward Lena. "Let's find out."

When Lily and Rachel reached Lena, she turned her back and tried to wipe the tears from her face.

She wears that same dress to school every day, Lily thought.

"Tell us what's wrong," Rachel said.

But Lena just shook her head.

"If you don't tell us, we'll tell Miss Pearson you were crying," Rachel said.

Lily looked at her friend. "Rachel, that's not nice."

"Well, are you going to tell us or not?" Rachel persisted.

"I have no money for the Pedestal Fund," Lena said quietly.

"How come?" Rachel asked in a softer tone.

Lena didn't reply.

Suddenly Lily remembered a day last month when she went with Mama to pick up her grandmother at the shop. She saw Lena bending over one of the many sewing machines in that big room. Grandma told her that Lena worked there to help support her family.

Lily looked at Lena's tear-streaked face. She reached up and touched the little purse. There was so much money inside. She unpinned the pin and opened the purse.

"Here, Lena," she said. "Here is forty cents for you." Lena looked at the forty cents in Lily's outstretched hand.

"Take it," Lily urged. "I have a lot more." She pulled out the two pennies Mrs. Rosen had given her. "Here's two cents more."

Lena took the money. "Thank you, Lily," she said.

"What did you do that for?" Rachel asked as they headed toward the main gate of the school.

Lily was silent. She was thinking about how she had felt last Friday when she had no money to give to the Pedestal Fund.

The first bell rang and children began forming lines in front of their teachers. The two girls stood in line before Miss Pearson. When everyone had gathered, the children filed silently into the school and to their classroom. Lily slipped quietly into her seat. There was a low buzz in the room until Miss Pearson signaled for silence.

"I think it best that we collect the money

for the Pedestal Fund at the beginning of the school day so there won't be any chance of losing it during recess." Miss Pearson stood before the blackboard with her chalk. "Please raise your hands if you have something to contribute."

"Sam?"

"Thirty cents, Miss Pearson."

Miss Pearson wrote 30 on the blackboard. She turned around and looked at the children. "Rachel?"

Rachel raced up the aisle. "Three dimes and a nickel!" she yelled.

Miss Pearson wrote 35 under the 30. She turned around again. "Lena?"

Lena walked up to the front of the class. "Forty-two cents," she said quietly.

When Miss Pearson called on Lily, Lily's heart gave a flutter. She unpinned the little purse from her dress, opened it, and let the money fall into her hand. Then she walked up the aisle and handed it to Miss Pearson. "Ninety-five cents," she said.

"Oh, my, how did you earn so much money, Lily?"

Rachel pulled the crown from inside her desk and put it on. "She made these," she said, pointing to her head.

Miss Pearson smiled. "Why, it looks just like Miss Liberty's crown. Was this your idea, Lily?"

"Yes, but my grandmother and mother helped me make them."

"Well, well, perhaps we can include a crown when we send our contributions for the Pedestal Fund to Mr. Pulitzer's newspaper."

Rachel handed her crown to Miss Pearson.

"Take this one," she said. "Lily can make me another."

First the children added all the numbers on the blackboard. Then they added together all the money they had earned last week.

Everyone clapped when they reached the total—seven dollars and forty-seven cents!

"Now we will write Mr. Pulitzer a letter," Miss Pearson said. "And maybe he will print it in his newspaper."

"Let's tell him that since the children of France helped to pay for the statue, we wanted to help pay for the pedestal," suggested Rachel.

Miss Pearson told the children that she would deliver the letter and the money and the crown to the newspaper herself.

That evening when everyone was sitting at the kitchen table having supper, Lily asked, "Grandma, do you remember that girl I know who works in your shop?"

Grandma paused for a moment. "Yes," she said, "Lena works in the shop every afternoon.

She threads the needles for the sewing machines."

"She's in my class at school," Lily said.

Mrs. Lafferty shook her head. "I thought she was older than you, Lily. I've heard that her family is very, very poor. She works to help feed her brothers and sisters."

"She didn't bring in any money for the Pedestal Fund. I gave her forty-two cents so she could give to the Pedestal Fund like everyone else."

Mama smiled. "Oh, Lily, that was a nice thing to do."

"When you said that freedom won't put food in poor people's mouths, did you mean someone like Lena?"

"Yes, Lily."

"Well, maybe Lena is poor but she loves Miss Liberty just as much as I do. I wish you loved her, too, Mama."

"If your mama doesn't care for the Statue of Liberty and you do, Lily, that's all right," Grandma said.

Papa smiled at Mama. "In this country freedom means that you are free to have different opinions. Isn't that right, Mama?"

Mama leaned over and patted Lily's hand. "Papa is right, Lily. And who knows, perhaps someday I will change my mind about Miss Liberty when I see her for myself."

6
The French Ship Arrives

❧

When Lily got home from school on Thursday, Mama was pushing Charlie back and forth in his carriage in front of their building.

"Guess what, Mama!" she exclaimed. "Miss Pearson said the French ship is here. She came yesterday!"

"I know," Mama replied. "And I have a surprise for you. The Knickerbocker Ice Company gave Papa three tickets to see the naval parade in the harbor tomorrow from their ship. He wants to know if you would like to ask someone to go with you."

"Don't you want to go?" Lily asked.

"No, Lily, it would be too hard to take Charlie, and Grandma can't go, either. She has to work."

"Then Rachel," Lily said quickly. "She

helped me sell all the crowns."

That night Lily was so excited she could hardly finish her supper.

"It took four weeks for the *Isère* to come from France to New York," Papa said. "It was a rough voyage. They ran out of coal during the last part of the trip and had to depend on their sails for power."

Lily looked worried. "Is Miss Liberty all right?" she asked.

"Oh, yes," Papa replied. "She's carefully packed in two hundred and thirteen crates."

"Lily," Mama said, "why don't you make a crown to wear for the celebration tomorrow."

Lily looked at her mother in surprise. Was Mama also excited about the celebration?

"I think I'll make one for Rachel, too."

"I will help you, Lily," Grandma said.

So after supper Grandma helped Lily cut out two more crowns.

Lily went to bed, sure she would never be able to fall asleep, but when she opened her eyes again it was morning. Papa was already at the kitchen table eating breakfast. She got out of bed and dressed quickly.

"Take along a sweater, Lily. It's always cooler on the water," Mama said. "And here is lunch for the three of you."

Lily gave Mama a hug.

"I know this is an exciting day for you, Lily." Mama smiled at her. "You look beautiful with your crown on."

Papa and Lily left their apartment, walked down the block a short distance, and crossed the street. Rachel was waiting outside her house for them.

"Here." Lily gave her the crown.

Rachel put it on. "Thank you, Lily," she said.

They walked over to Eighth Street and Broadway to take one of the horse-drawn streetcars that ran between Broadway and South Ferry.

Lily and Rachel sat together looking out of the window. Flags were flying from all the buildings along lower Broadway. Long streamers of red, white, and blue swung to and fro, waving a welcome.

"Look at Liberty's crown," said a lady to her companion.

"Where did you get them?" she asked the two girls.

"She made them," Rachel said, pointing at Lily.

"Well, well, you're in the spirit of things, aren't you?" said a man who sat across from them.

When they reached South Ferry, there was already a huge crowd of people milling about.

"Take my hands, girls. I don't want to lose you," Papa said.

The picnic basket banged against her legs as Lily struggled to hold onto Papa with her other hand.

Papa pushed his way toward the dock. By nine-thirty, they had boarded the A.C. *Cheney* and found a spot on the upper deck. Twenty minutes later, the steamship packed with people made its way to the middle of the harbor to await the arrival of the French ship.

"Now stay right here, girls. I'm going below," Papa said.

Lily and Rachel leaned over the railing of the A.C. *Cheney* and looked out on the harbor. There were so many boats! Big boats

and little ones, all decorated with flags! It was a wonder they didn't bump into one another. They could hear bands playing on the big side-wheelers. On deck just behind them a man played "Yankee Doodle" on his accordion.

Rachel pointed. "That's Bedloe's Island, where the statue is going to be if they ever finish the pedestal."

"I wish she were standing there now," Lily said wistfully.

"When is the ship coming? I hope we don't have to wait around forever," Rachel said.

Suddenly there was the sound of cannon fire. A cheer went up from the passengers.

"She's leaving Sandy Hook!" yelled someone. "That's the cannon from the fort."

Rachel straightened her crown. "I'm hungry," she said. "What did you bring for lunch?"

Lily stared at her friend. How could she think of food at a time like this? "We have to wait for Papa," she said.

"Can I just look?" asked Rachel.

"I guess so." Lily opened the basket and both girls peered inside. Lily could see slices of Mama's bread and cheese and something wrapped in paper. She guessed it was cake.

Rachel reached into the basket. "Let's have an apple."

Suddenly there was more cannon fire. Then more. Boom. Boom.

"What's happening?" Lily asked anxiously.

"She's coming into the channel! They're saluting her from Fort Hamilton and Fort Wadsworth," said a woman next to them.

Lily and Rachel leaned over the railing, straining to see.

Just then Mr. Lafferty appeared. "There she is!" he shouted.

Lily saw a great white ship decorated with hundreds of gaily colored flags.

Now the noise was deafening. All the boats in the harbor were tooting horns and blowing their steam whistles. Lily could see fire spitting out of the cannon on Bedloe's Island. She put her fingers in her ears.

People were shouting and cheering on all the boats as the *Isère* drew closer and closer. The French sailors standing on her deck were waving their hats. Lily and Rachel took off their crowns and waved them, too. Then the ladies on all the big boats nearby began waving their handkerchiefs. It looked like a snow-storm!

"Bonjour! Bonjour!" Rachel yelled.

At last the *Isère* reached Bedloe's Island. Lily could see the ship's anchor's chain being let down into the water.

Rachel put her crown back on. "When are we going to eat?"

Mr. Lafferty reached into the basket and pulled out the lunch Mama had made for them. "We can sit right down here on the deck," he said.

Lily ate her lunch in silence. She was thinking about Miss Liberty and how sad it was that she couldn't see the big celebration in her honor. How much longer would she have to lie hidden away in boxes at the bottom of the big white ship?

7
Liberty Enlightening the World

❦

It was late afternoon when Lily and Rachel and Papa finally returned home. After saying good-bye to Rachel, they climbed the stairs to their apartment.

Mama greeted them at the door. "Well, well, Lily, what was it like out there?"

"So many ships, Mama, and the most beautiful of all was the *Isère!* She was all white!" Then Lily told Mama about the booming cannons and whistles blowing and everyone cheering when the French ship came into the harbor.

"I've never seen anything like it!" Papa exclaimed. "There were so many ships in the parade, Mama!"

"May I go outside and wait for Grandma?" Lily asked.

"Yes, Lily. Supper isn't ready yet," Mama replied.

Lily sat down on the front steps. Grandma was not yet in sight. But she could see Mr. Ames approaching on his street sprinkler. When he reached Lily, he stopped.

"You like that statue, eh?"

"Oh, yes, Mr. Ames. I love Miss Liberty!"

"I suppose she will be quite a sight out there in the harbor someday. Maybe I'll give a little money to the Pedestal Fund. Giddap!" He slapped the reins of his horse.

"That's a good idea, Mr. Ames!" Lily said.

Just then a window opened behind her.

"Lily! So you went to the celebration! I could hear the cannon. Such a loud noise! Was there a big crowd? Did you see the French ship?"

Lily waited until Mrs. Rosen paused for breath. "It was very exciting, Mrs. Rosen. The French ship was all white and it was decorated with flags. And bands played and—"

Mrs. Rosen interrupted her. "I knew I should have gone. I told myself, Etty, you're going to miss something big, something important."

Maybe Mrs. Rosen has changed her mind about Miss Liberty, too, Lily thought.

"I think I will give a little money. The sooner I can see that statue the better!" And Mrs. Rosen closed the window.

A wagon stopped in front of Lily's building. "Hey, weren't you the little girl selling crowns?" asked the driver.

"Yes," Lily replied.

"Got any left?"

"No, but I can make some more," Lily said.

"I'll take three. I'll come by tomorrow." And the wagon rolled off down the street.

Soon another carriage stopped. This time a woman leaned out of the carriage window. "Where are the crowns?" she asked.

"I sold them all," Lily said. "If you come back tomorrow, I'll have some more."

"Good!" The woman withdrew her head from the window and the carriage slowly moved on.

At last Lily saw her grandmother coming up the street. She ran to greet her. "Grandma, everybody wants to buy a crown! What are we going to do?" she asked.

"I'm not surprised, Lily, after seeing the paper today."

Lily looked puzzled.

"I have the paper here. I'll show you when we get home."

As soon as Lily and Grandma entered the kitchen, Grandma spread the newspaper on the table.

"Look at that!" she said, pointing to the right-hand page.

Lily leaned over and tried to see what Grandma was pointing at. There was a picture of the crown she had made and the letter her class had sent to Mr. Pulitzer!

"Read it out loud, Lily," Mama said.

" 'Dear Mr. Pulitzer,

Here is seven dollars and forty-seven cents. We wanted to help pay for Miss Liberty's pedestal because the schoolchildren of France helped to pay for the statue. We worked hard. Everyone in our class gave some money.

Sincerely,
Miss Pearson's class, P.S. 19

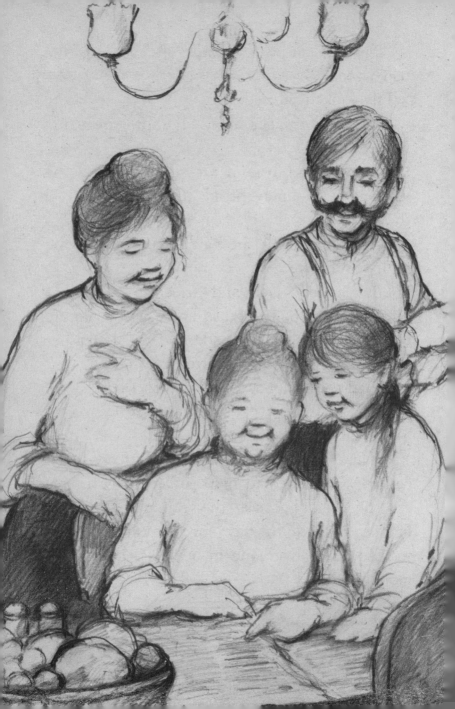

" 'P.S. The crown was made by Lily Lafferty. She sold a lot of them to help pay for the pedestal. We hope you will wear it to work.' "

"Lily, I'll help you make more crowns. Maybe the ladies in the shop will help, too," Grandma said.

"Imagine that!" Mama exclaimed. "Your name in that big newspaper. Everyone will see it. I'm so proud of you!"

"We will keep the paper," Papa said. "When you grow up and have children of your own, you can show them that you helped to build Miss Liberty's pedestal," Papa said.

"Do you really think we will raise enough money to build the pedestal, Papa?" Lily asked.

"Everybody is excited about the statue now that Miss Liberty has arrived. I'm sure that in a few more weeks we will have all the money."

"Once we raise the money for the statue, I hope we will begin to pay attention to our poor people," said Mama.

Lily straightened her crown. Suddenly she

picked up the newspaper and climbed up onto a kitchen chair.

"What are you doing, Lily?" asked Mama.

Lily reached over and took the salt shaker from the table and held it high in her right hand. She put her left foot forward and her right foot back.

"Oh, Lily, I can guess!" Papa laughed.

Yes, she was the biggest statue ever built! She was taller than any building in the whole city of New York. She was a queen. And her name was Liberty, Liberty Enlightening the World!

Afterword

❧

The big celebration in honor of Miss Liberty's arrival from France on the *Isère* was held on June 19, 1885. A month later, all the money needed to complete the pedestal had been raised.

Mr. Pulitzer, the publisher of the *World*, had promised to print in his newspaper the name of every person who donated any money to the Pedestal Fund, and he did. Lily read that Mrs. Rosen contributed fifty cents and Mr. Ames gave a dollar.

It took almost a year to complete the pedestal. Then workmen began to put together the great statue piece by piece.

One Sunday, the Laffertys took the ferry out to Bedloe's Island to see the work in progress. Lily stood next to one of Miss Liberty's toes. It was bigger than Lily!

Almost a year and a half later, on October

28, 1886, *Liberty Enlightening the World* was finally ready to be unveiled. On that day her face was covered by a gigantic French flag. After the statue was formally presented to the United States by France, Mr. Bartholdi, the sculptor, pulled a cord and the flag dropped to the ground. Once again, cannons roared and whistles blew all over the harbor. Then President Cleveland made a speech thanking the French people for their generous gift and accepting the statue on behalf of the American people.

This time Lily was not on a boat watching the ceremony. She stood with her family at Battery Park looking out at Bedloe's Island. Lily had waited a long time to see the Statue of Liberty standing in the harbor. She was not disappointed. Yes, Miss Liberty was beautiful!

How to Make
Miss Liberty's Crown:

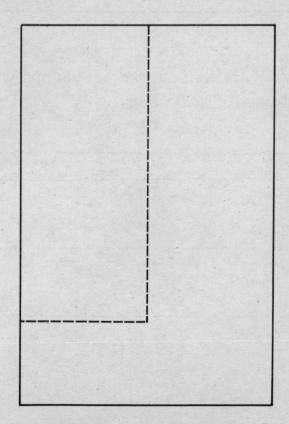

*T*ake a sheet of construction paper 12 x 18 inches. Cut a strip 14 inches long and 6 inches wide.

Turn your paper strip so that it looks like this:

Measure 2½ inches from the bottom and draw a pencil line straight across.

Fold your paper in half with the pencil line still showing on the outside.

Now comes the hard part—making the 7 rays of Miss Liberty's crown. Get a ruler and draw lines to make 3½ triangles with your pencil like this:

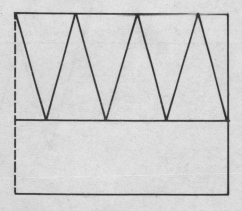

The first triangle should be half as wide as the other three. That's because it is on the fold. When you unfold the paper it will be a full-sized triangle. Don't worry if you don't get the triangles right the first time. Erase and try again until the three full-sized rays look about the same. Now cut on the lines you drew. Open your paper and you will have a crown. But wait! You are not finished yet. Fold the rays down over the band so that they are no longer sticking straight up. This will make them extend out from your head.

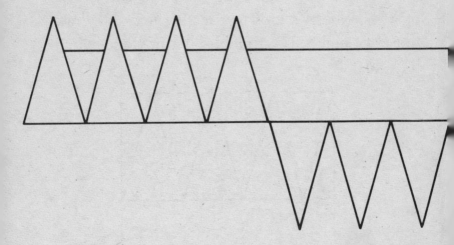

Finally, get two pieces of string each about 16 inches long. Make a knot at one end of each string. Then staple the knotted end to the band. The knot should keep the string from slipping out.

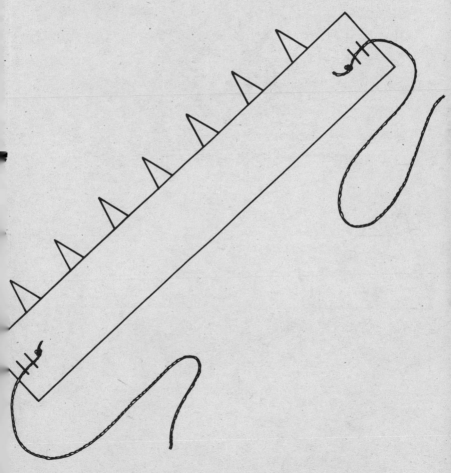

Put your crown on, tying the ends of the string together. Now look in the mirror. You are wearing a crown just like the one Lily made!

CARLA STEVENS has written more than a dozen books for children, among them, *Anna, Grandpa and the Big Storm* and *Trouble for Lucy.* She teaches creative writing at the New School for Social Research in New York City.

DEBORAH KOGAN RAY, a painter, illustrator, and writer, has received many awards for her illustrated children's books, including the Drexel Citation. Ms. Ray has two grown daughters and divides her time between residences in Philadelphia and Eastport, Maine.